SUPERMAN® FAMILY ADVENTURES™

STONE ARCH BOOKS
a capstone imprint

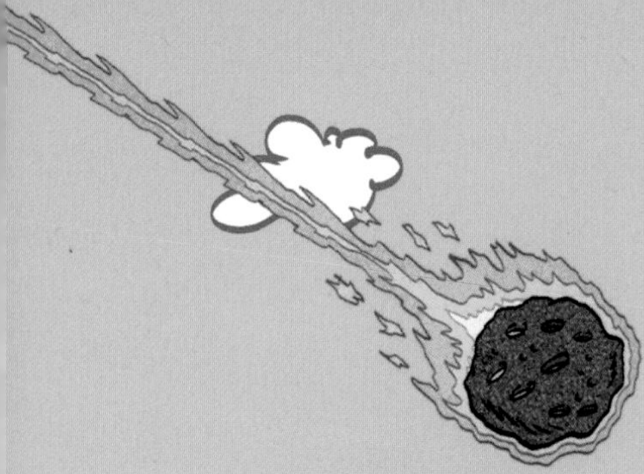

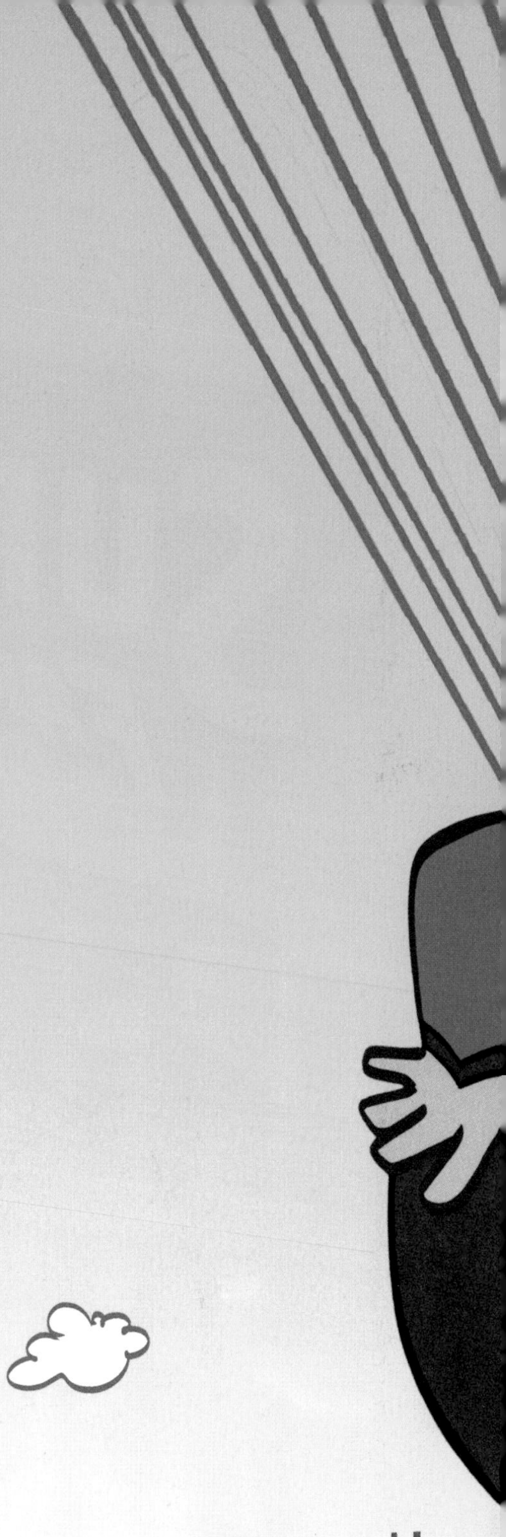

STONE ARCH BOOKS®

Published in 2014
A Capstone Imprint
1710 Roe Crest Drive
North Mankato, MN 56003
www.capstonepub.com

Originally published by DC Comics in the U.S. in single
magazine form as SUPERMAN FAMILY ADVENTURES #12.

DC Comics
1700 Broadway, New York, NY 10019
A Warner Bros. Entertainment Company

Cataloging-in-Publication Data is available at the
Library of Congress website:
ISBN: 978-1-4342-9005-2 (library binding)

Summary: The return of the lunch lady! Er, we mean, the return of DARKSEID! Has he come back for good--or evil?

STONE ARCH BOOKS
Ashley C. Andersen Zantop Publisher
Michael Dahl Editorial Director
Donald Lemke & Sean Tulien Editors
Brann Garvey & Russell Griesmer Designers
Kathy McColley Production Specialist

DC COMICS
Kristy Quinn Original U.S. Editor

Printed in the United States of America in Stevens Point, Wisconsin.
102014 008565R

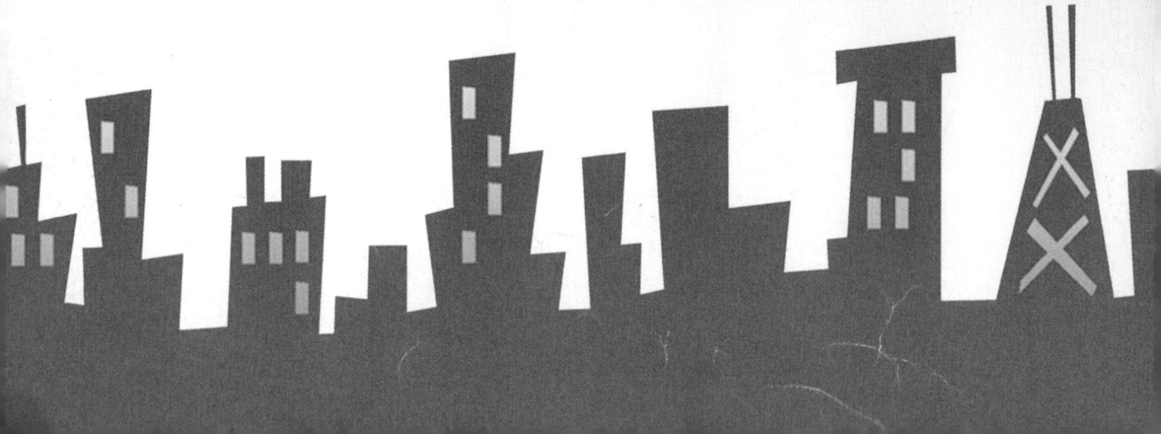

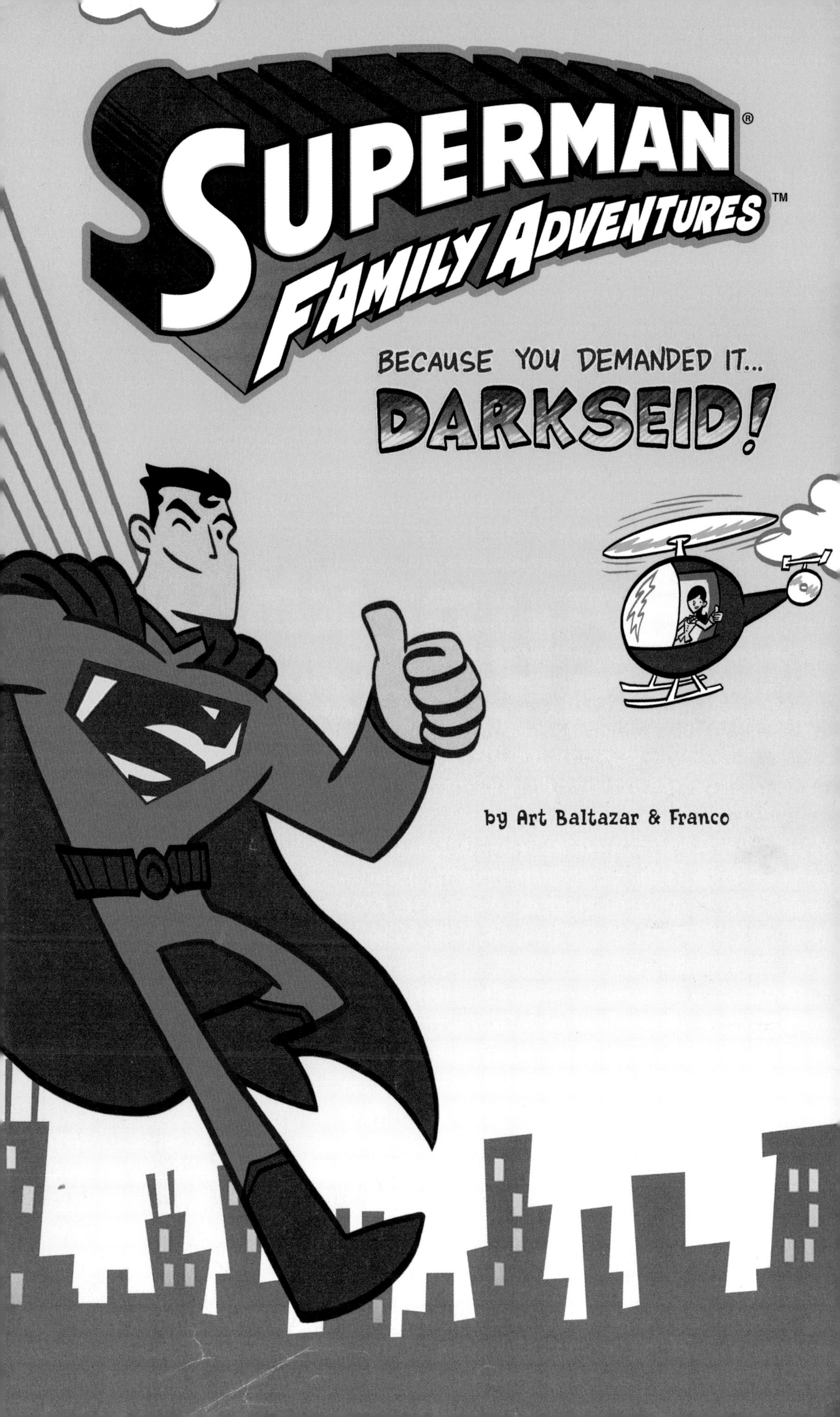
SUPERMAN® FAMILY ADVENTURES™
BECAUSE YOU DEMANDED IT...
DARKSEID!
by Art Baltazar & Franco

SUPERMAN® FAMILY ADVENTURES™

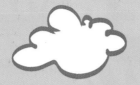

MEANWHILE IN THE FAR REACHES OF **SPACE**...

A **FIERY** METEORITE **IS** GOING TO DESTROY THE **EARTH!**

IT'S TRUE.

NOTHING CAN **STOP IT!**

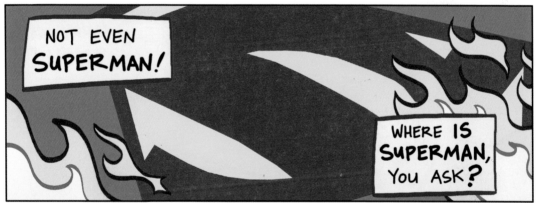

NOT EVEN **SUPERMAN!**

WHERE **IS** SUPERMAN, YOU ASK?

LET'S TAKE A CLOSER LOOK AT THAT **FIERY METEORITE,** SHALL WE?

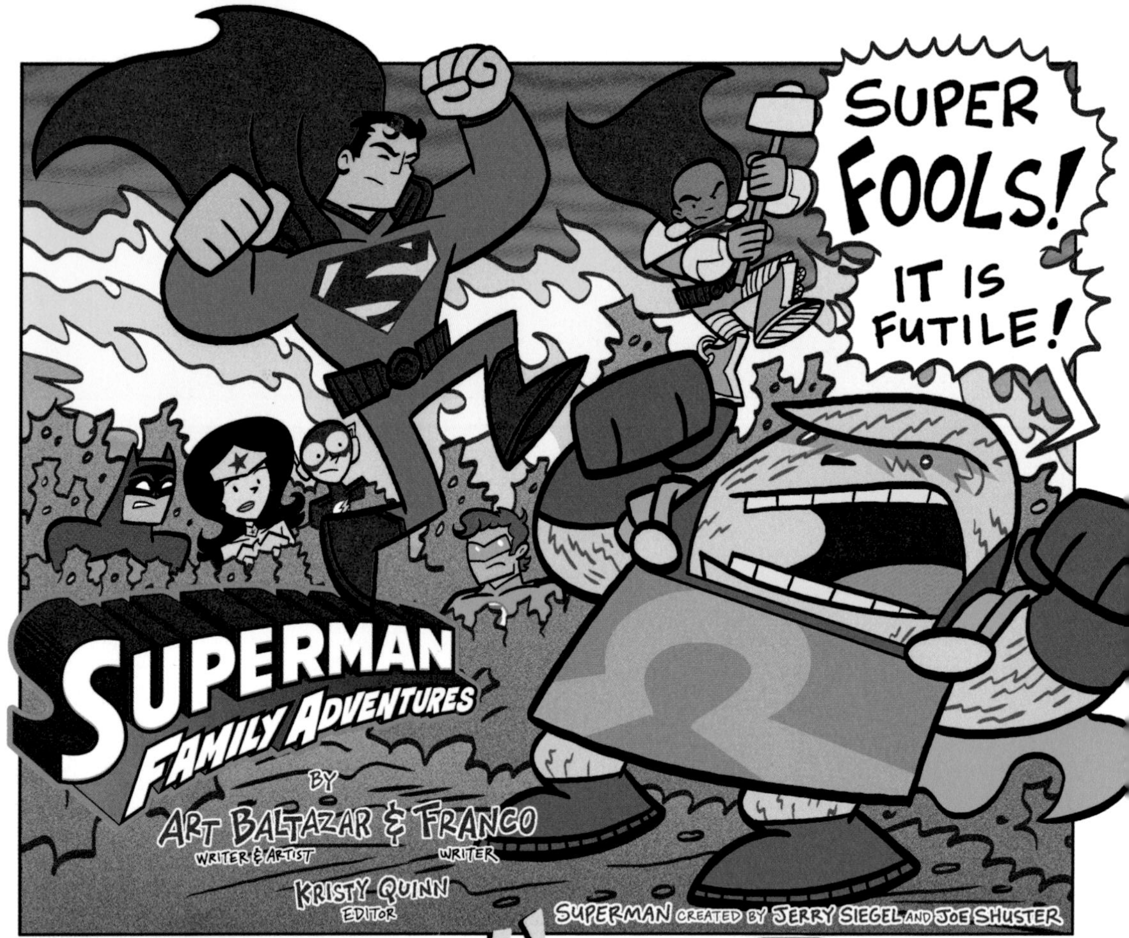
SUPER FOOLS! IT IS FUTILE!
SUPERMAN FAMILY ADVENTURES
BY
ART BALTAZAR & FRANCO
WRITER & ARTIST
WRITER
KRISTY QUINN
EDITOR
SUPERMAN CREATED BY JERRY SIEGEL AND JOE SHUSTER

SUPERBOY CREATED BY JERRY SIEGEL.

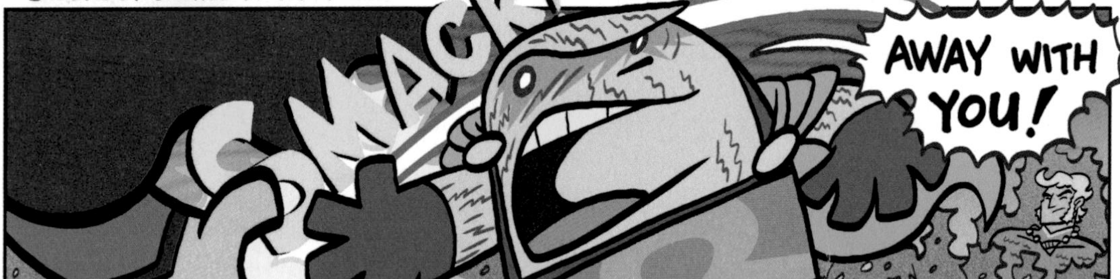
SMACK!
AWAY WITH YOU!

SUPERGIRL BASED ON CHARACTERS CREATED BY JERRY SIEGEL AND JOE SHUSTER. BY SPECIAL ARRANGEMENT WITH THE JERRY SIEGEL FAMILY.

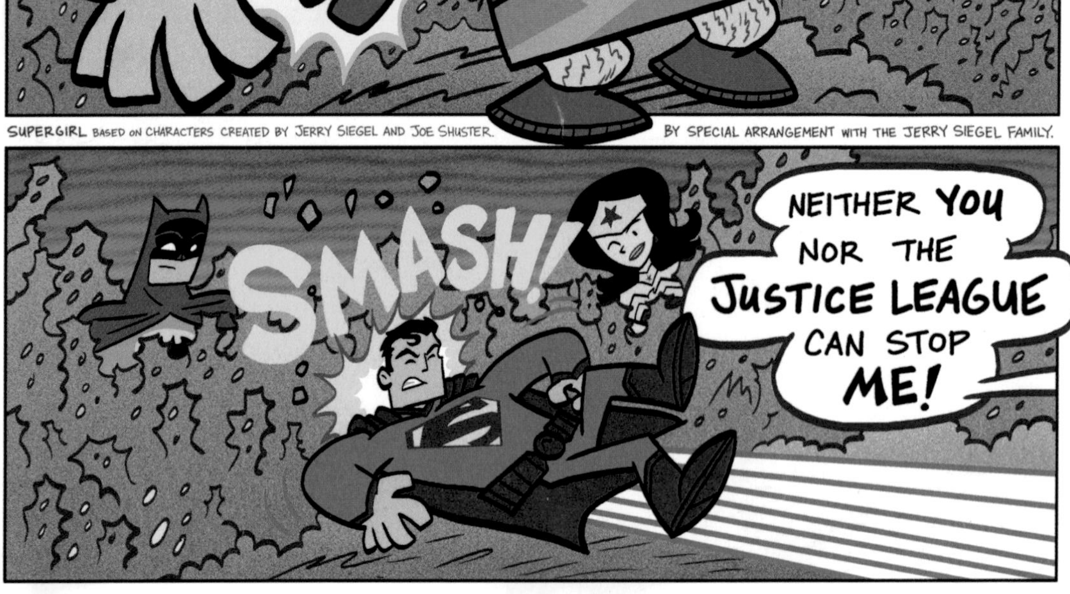
SMASH!
NEITHER YOU NOR THE JUSTICE LEAGUE CAN STOP ME!

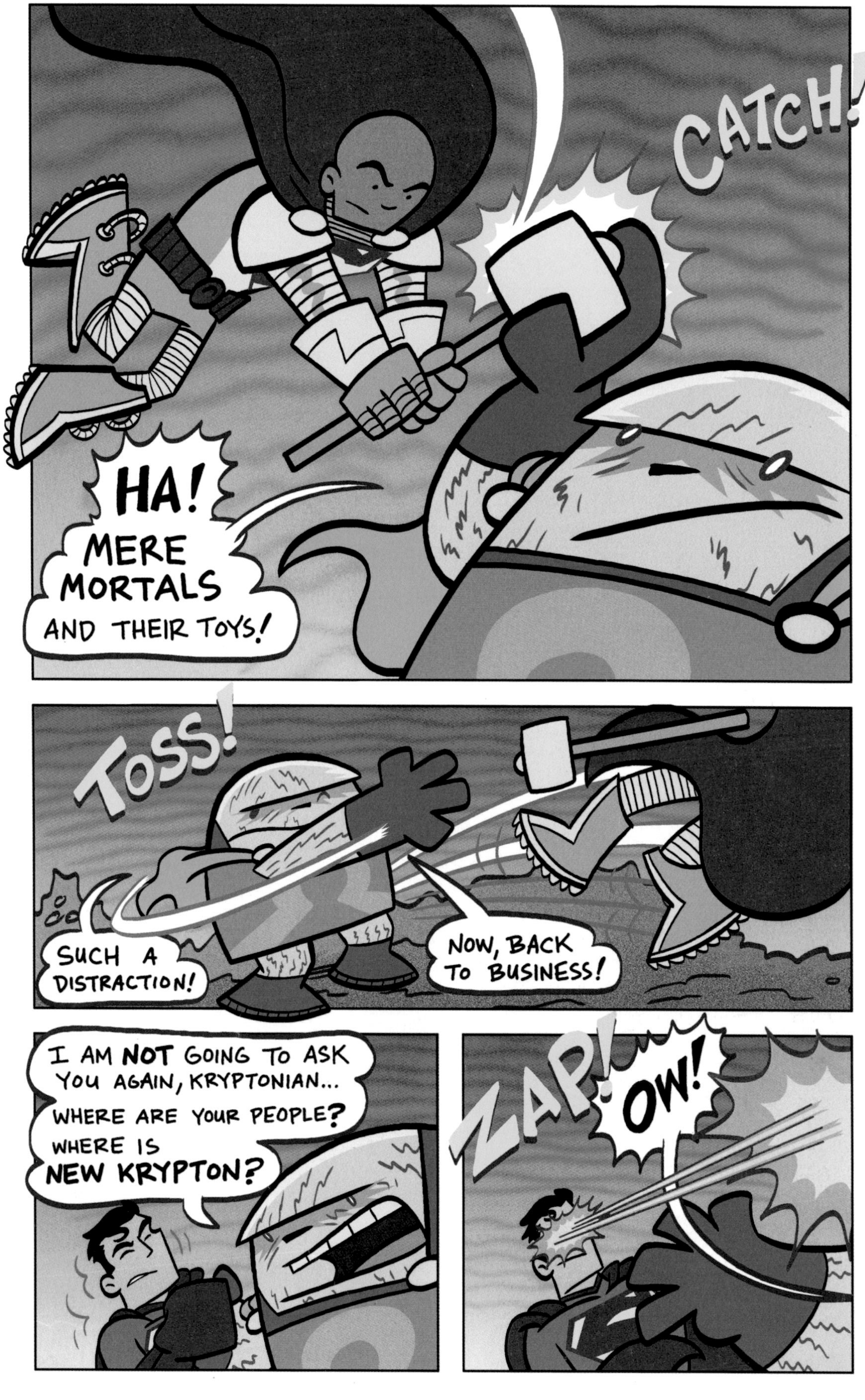
CATCH!
HA!
MERE MORTALS AND THEIR TOYS!
TOSS!
SUCH A DISTRACTION!
NOW, BACK TO BUSINESS!
I AM NOT GOING TO ASK YOU AGAIN, KRYPTONIAN...
WHERE ARE YOUR PEOPLE?
WHERE IS NEW KRYPTON?
ZAP!
OW!

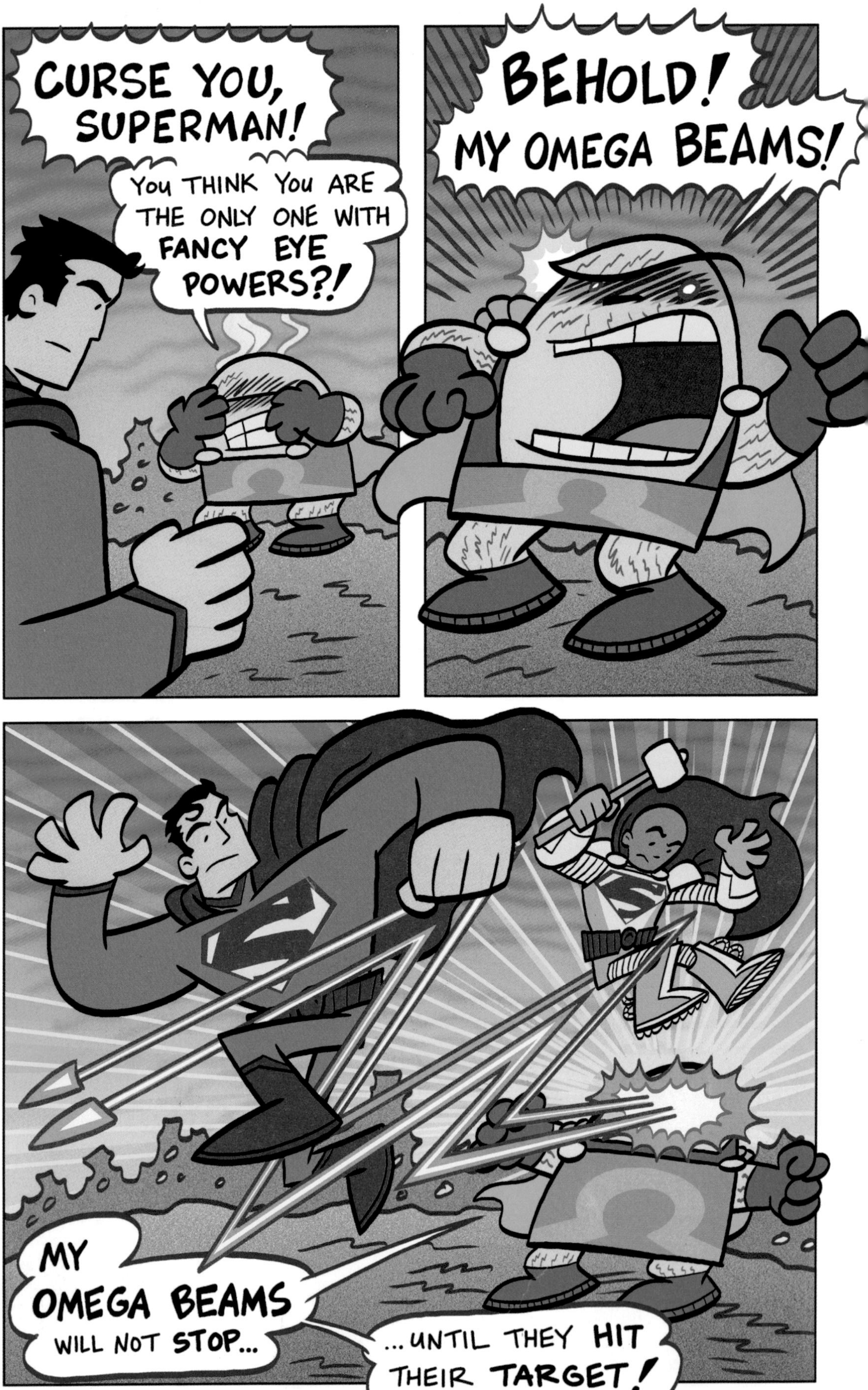
CURSE YOU, SUPERMAN!
YOU THINK YOU ARE THE ONLY ONE WITH FANCY EYE POWERS?!
BEHOLD! MY OMEGA BEAMS!
MY OMEGA BEAMS WILL NOT STOP...
...UNTIL THEY HIT THEIR TARGET!

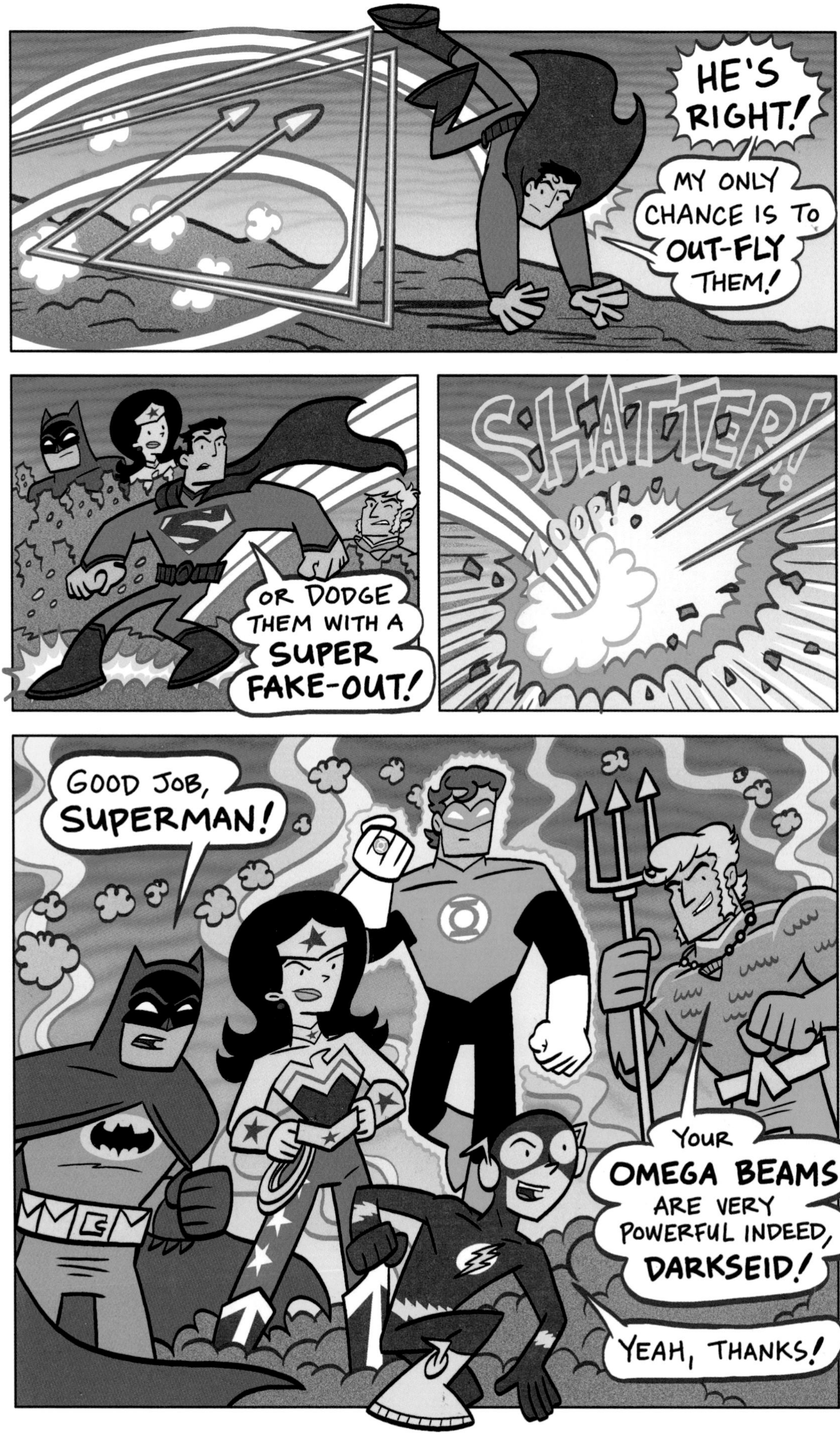
HE'S RIGHT!
MY ONLY CHANCE IS TO OUT-FLY THEM!
OR DODGE THEM WITH A SUPER FAKE-OUT!
SHATTER!
ZOOP!
GOOD JOB, SUPERMAN!
YOUR OMEGA BEAMS ARE VERY POWERFUL INDEED, DARKSEID!
YEAH, THANKS!

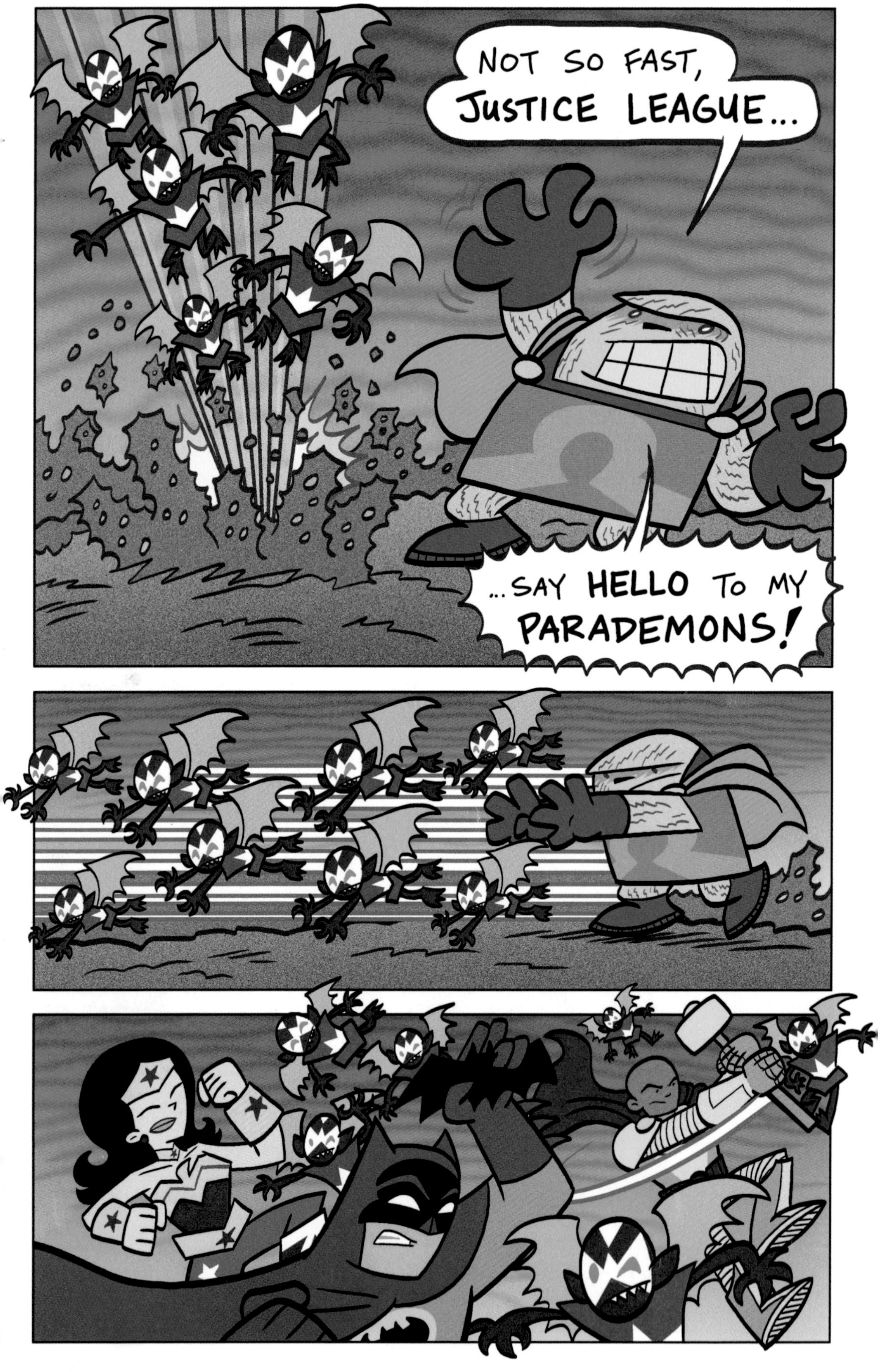
NOT SO FAST, JUSTICE LEAGUE...
...SAY HELLO TO MY PARADEMONS!

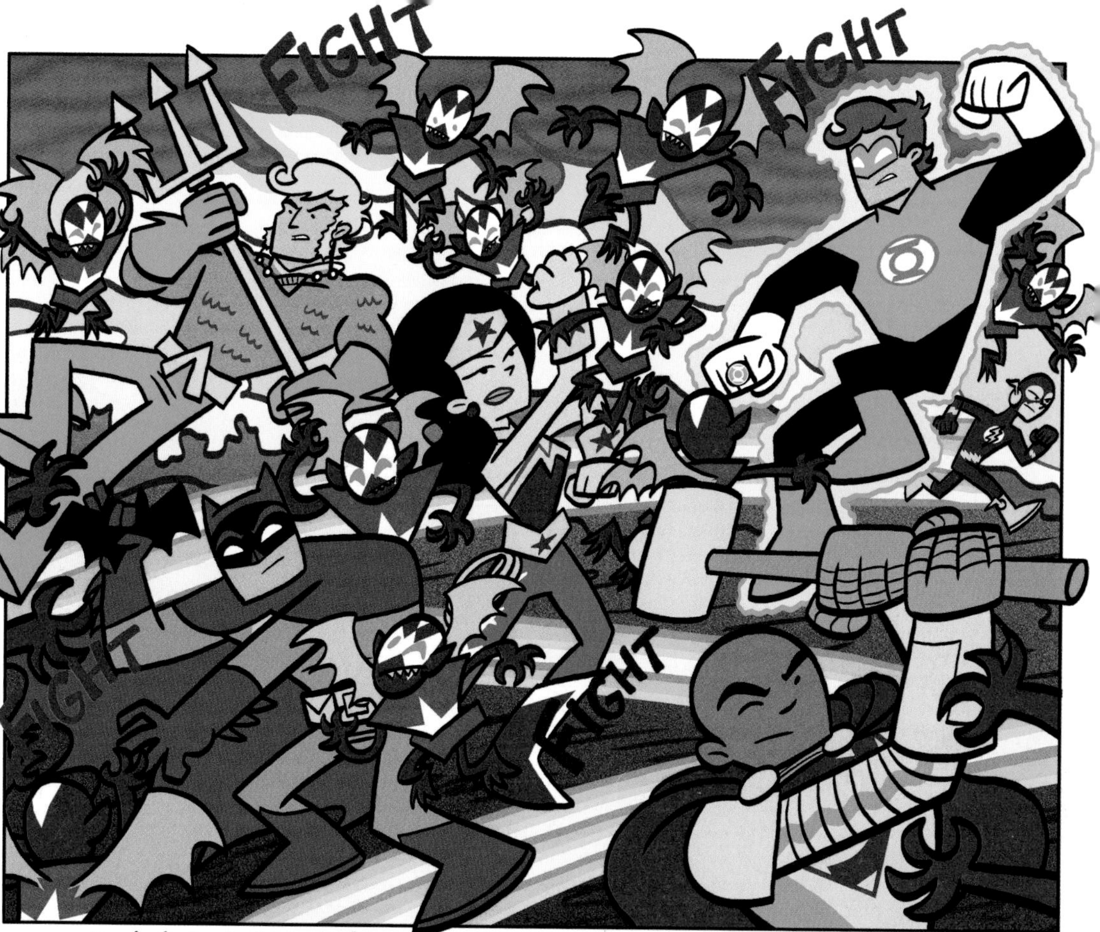

FIGHT
FIGHT
FIGHT
FIGHT

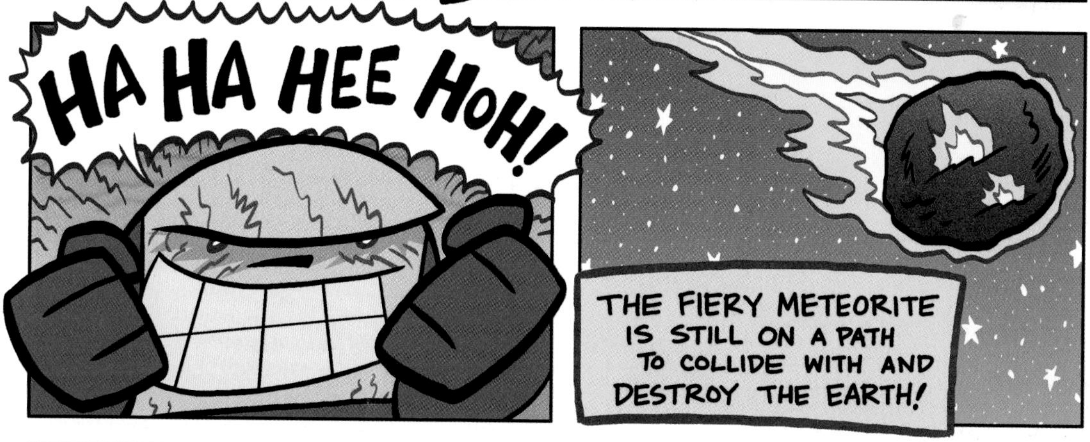

HA HA HEE HOH!
THE FIERY METEORITE IS STILL ON A PATH TO COLLIDE WITH AND DESTROY THE EARTH!

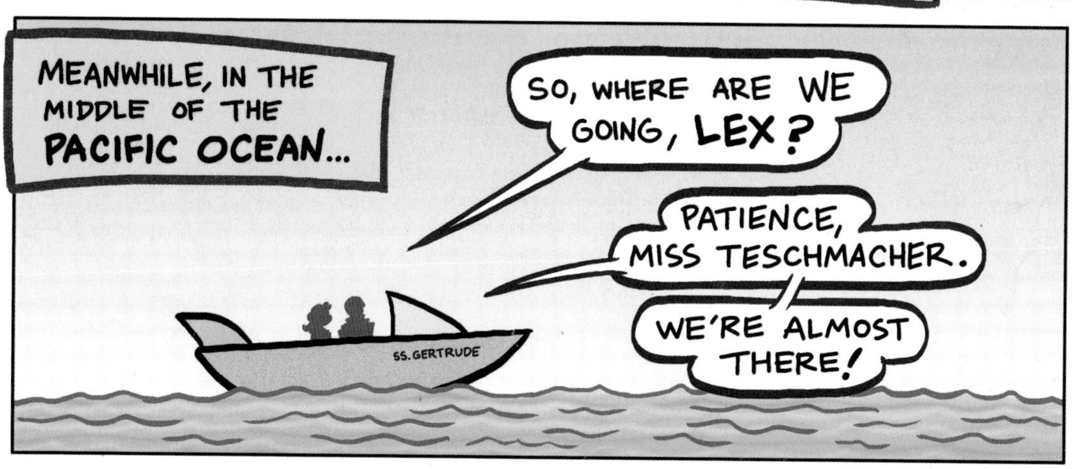

MEANWHILE, IN THE MIDDLE OF THE PACIFIC OCEAN...
SO, WHERE ARE WE GOING, LEX?
PATIENCE, MISS TESCHMACHER.
WE'RE ALMOST THERE!
SS. GERTRUDE

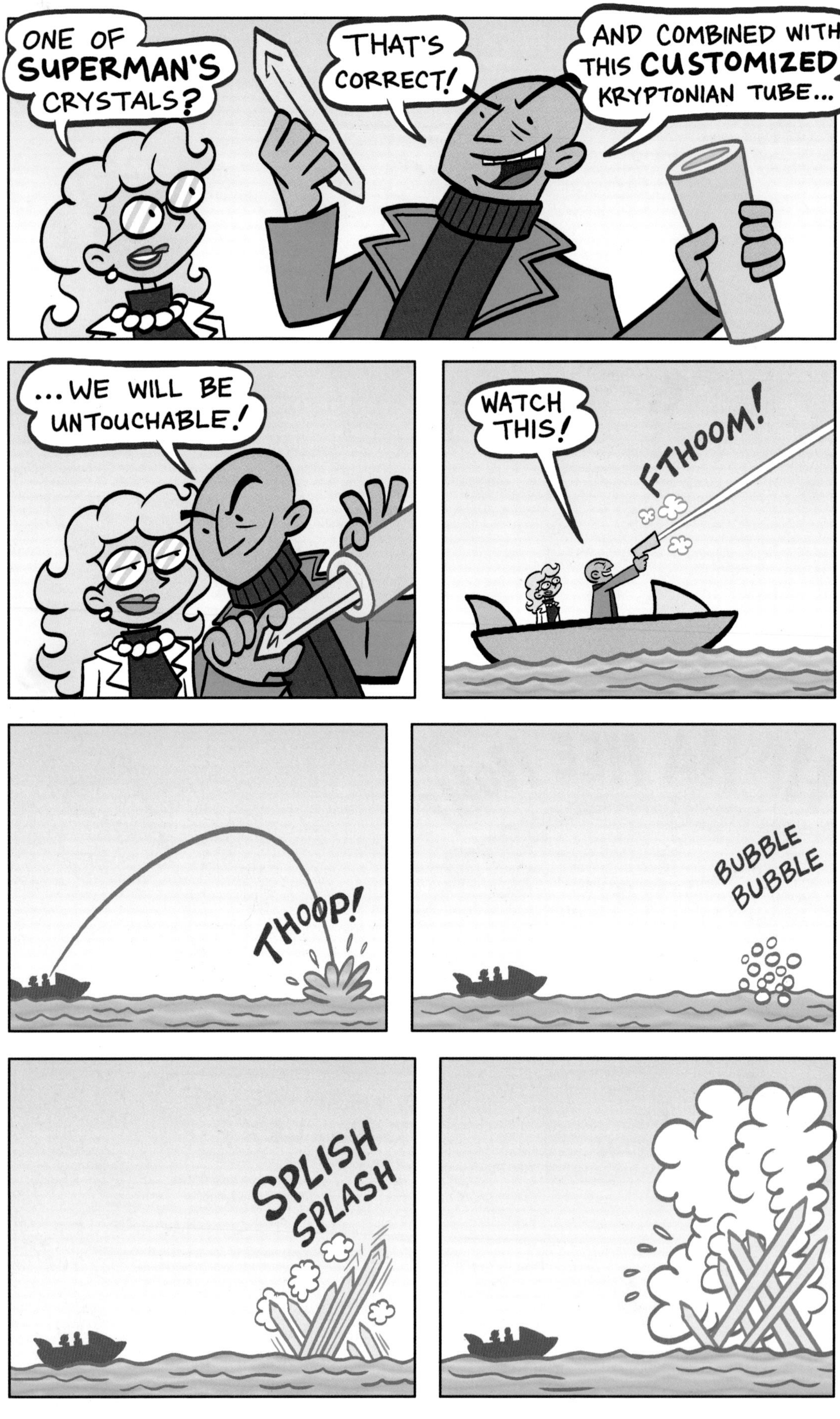
ONE OF SUPERMAN'S CRYSTALS?
THAT'S CORRECT!
AND COMBINED WITH THIS CUSTOMIZED KRYPTONIAN TUBE...
...WE WILL BE UNTOUCHABLE!
WATCH THIS!
FTHOOM!
THOOP!
BUBBLE BUBBLE
SPLISH SPLASH

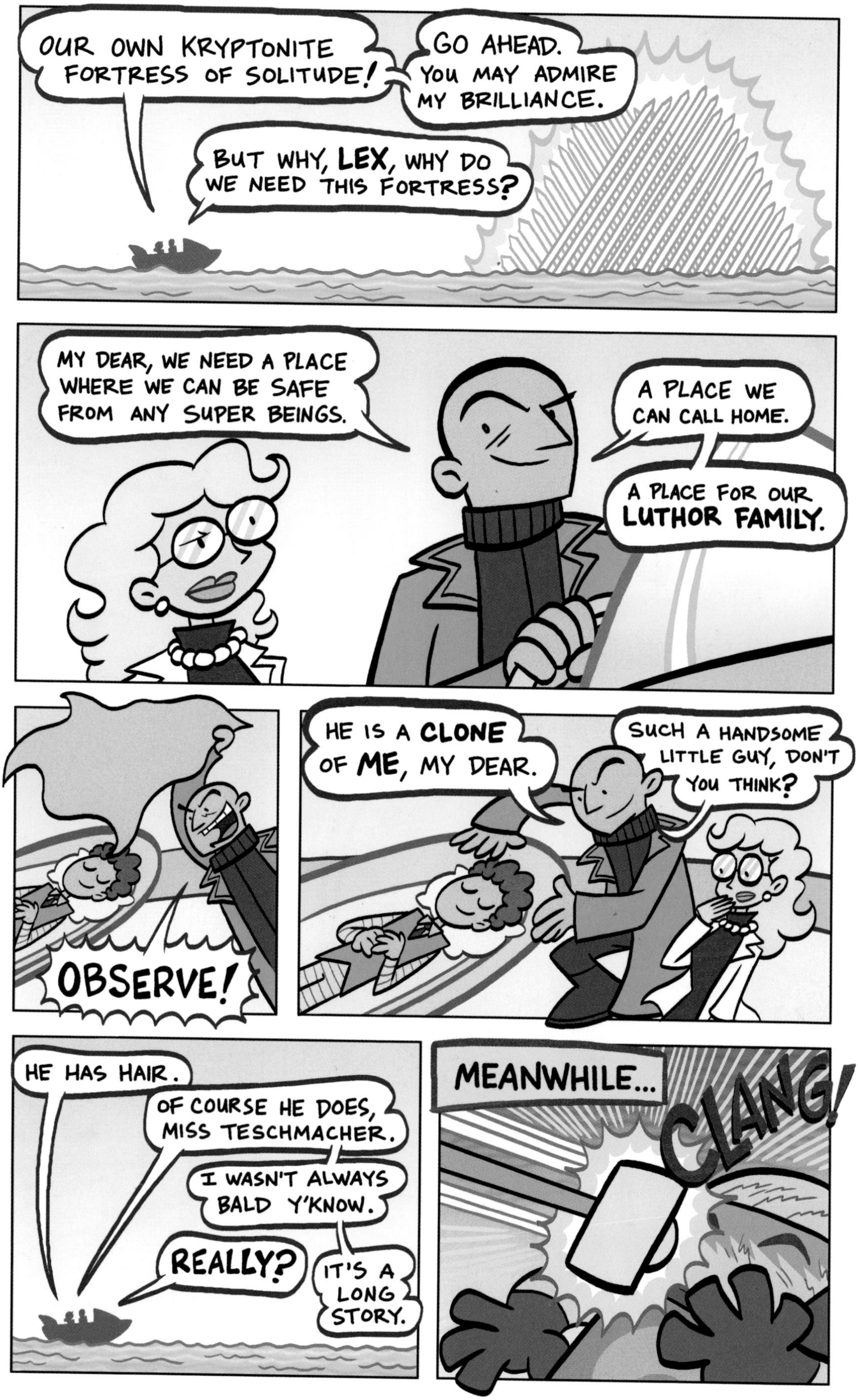

OUR OWN KRYPTONITE FORTRESS OF SOLITUDE!
GO AHEAD. YOU MAY ADMIRE MY BRILLIANCE.
BUT WHY, LEX, WHY DO WE NEED THIS FORTRESS?
MY DEAR, WE NEED A PLACE WHERE WE CAN BE SAFE FROM ANY SUPER BEINGS.
A PLACE WE CAN CALL HOME.
A PLACE FOR OUR LUTHOR FAMILY.
OBSERVE!
HE IS A CLONE OF ME, MY DEAR.
SUCH A HANDSOME LITTLE GUY, DON'T YOU THINK?
HE HAS HAIR.
OF COURSE HE DOES, MISS TESCHMACHER.
I WASN'T ALWAYS BALD Y'KNOW.
REALLY?
IT'S A LONG STORY.
MEANWHILE...
CLANG!

WOOOSH!

PUNCH!

GRAB!

SLAM!

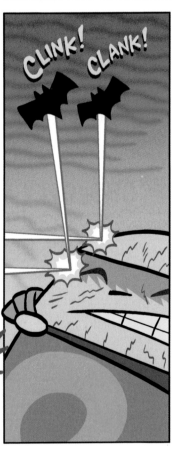

CLINK!

CLANK!

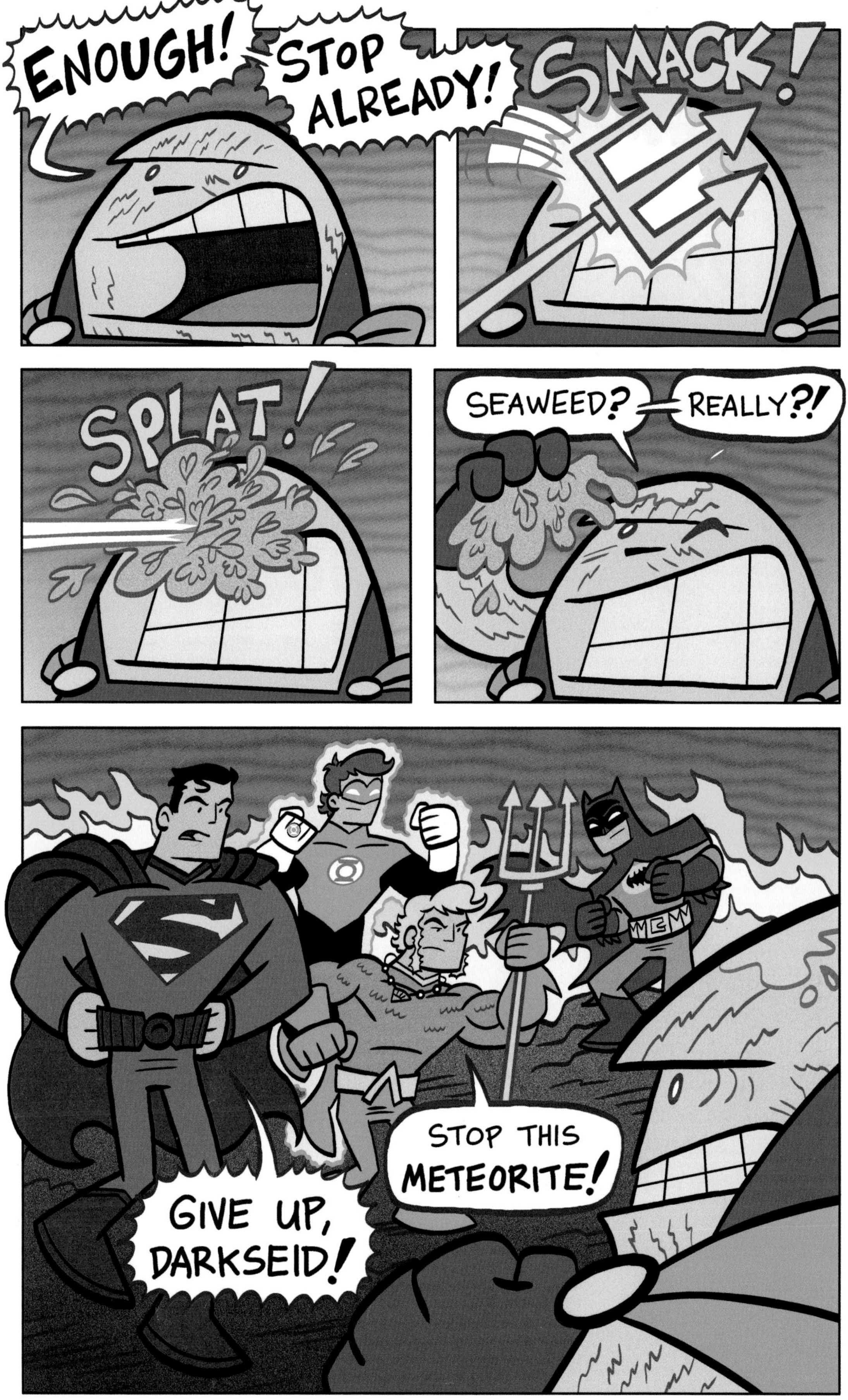
ENOUGH!
STOP ALREADY!
SMACK!
SPLAT!
SEAWEED?
REALLY?!
GIVE UP, DARKSEID!
STOP THIS METEORITE!

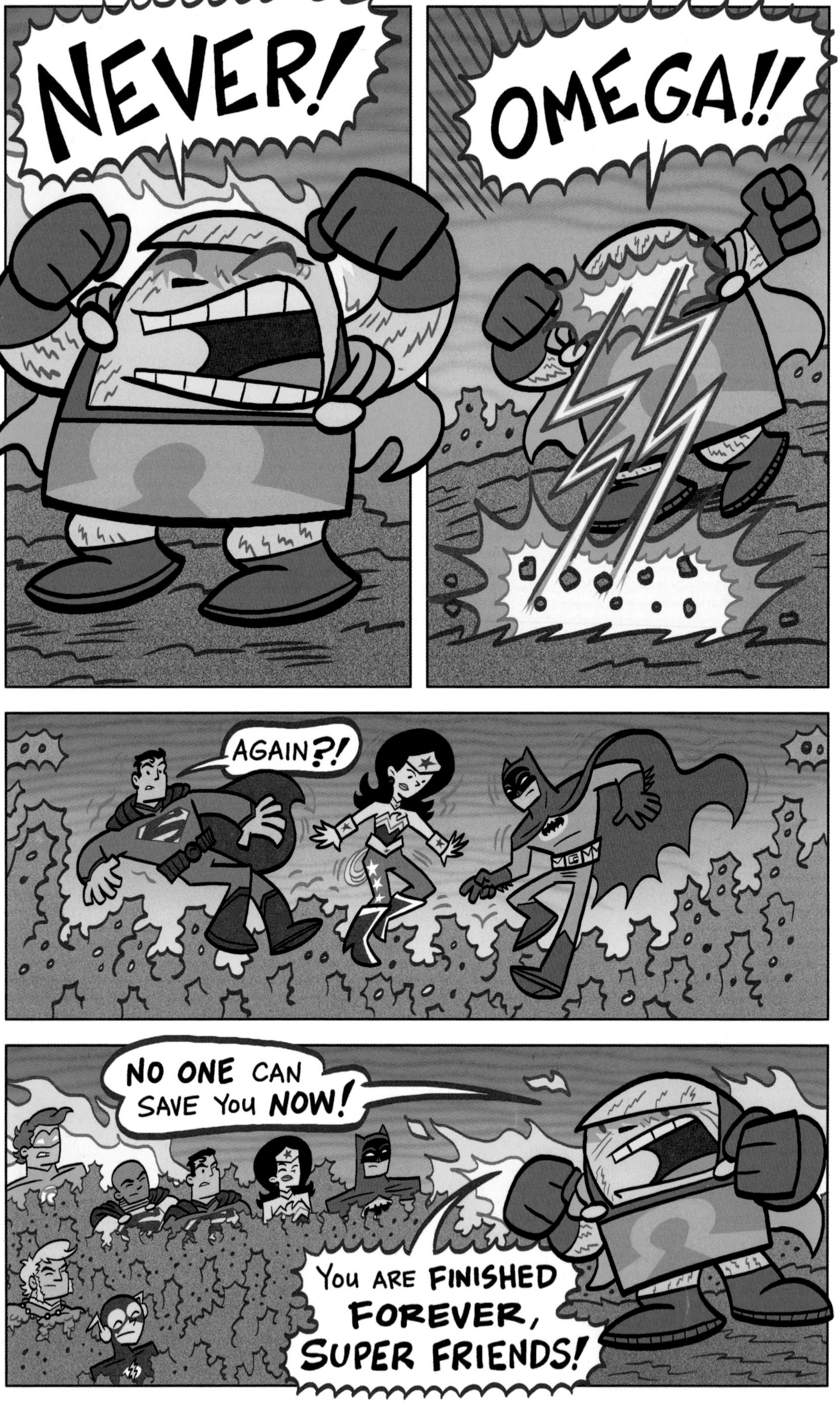
NEVER!
OMEGA!!
AGAIN?!
NO ONE CAN SAVE YOU NOW!
YOU ARE FINISHED FOREVER, SUPER FRIENDS!

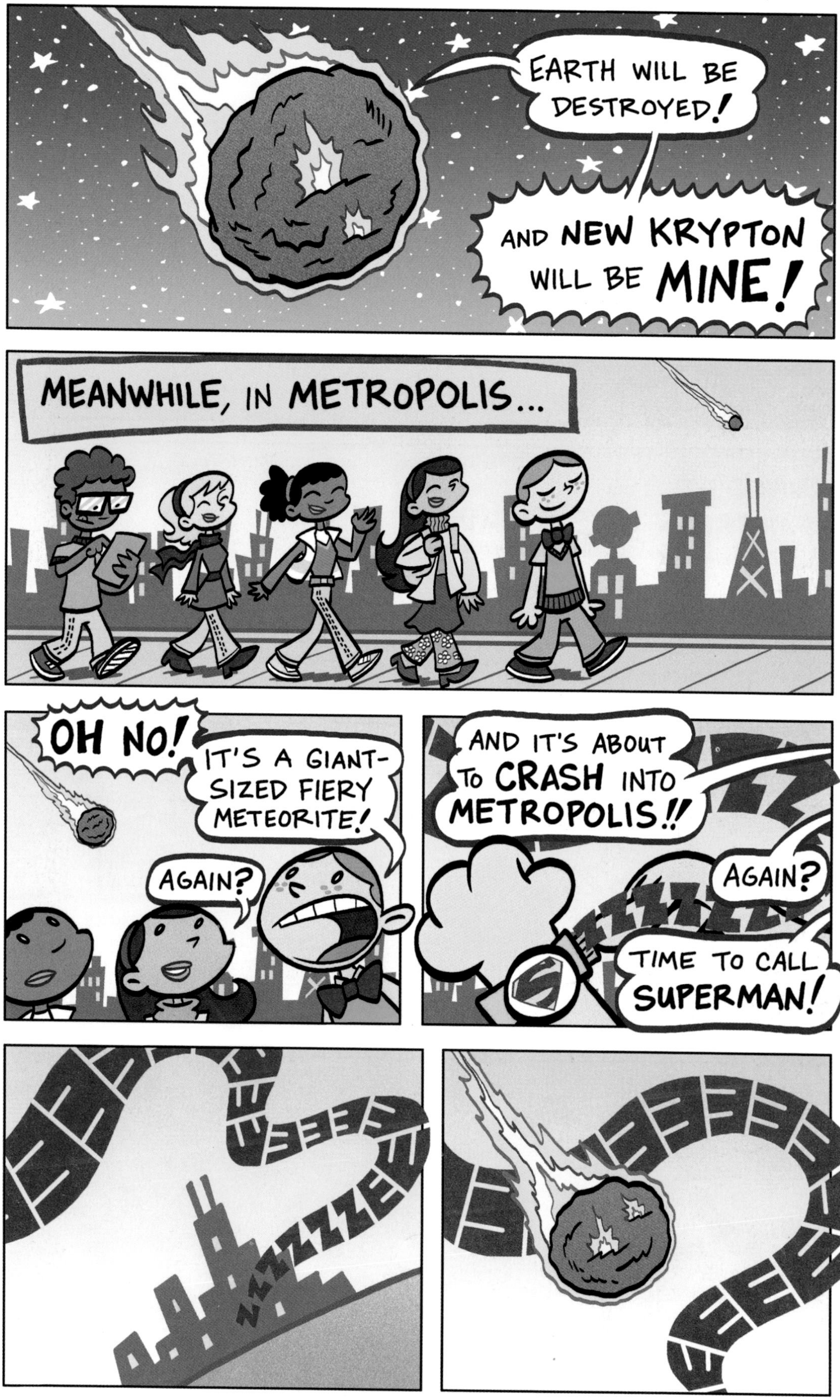

EARTH WILL BE DESTROYED!
AND NEW KRYPTON WILL BE MINE!
MEANWHILE, IN METROPOLIS...
OH NO!
IT'S A GIANT-SIZED FIERY METEORITE!
AGAIN?
AND IT'S ABOUT TO CRASH INTO METROPOLIS!!
AGAIN?
TIME TO CALL SUPERMAN!

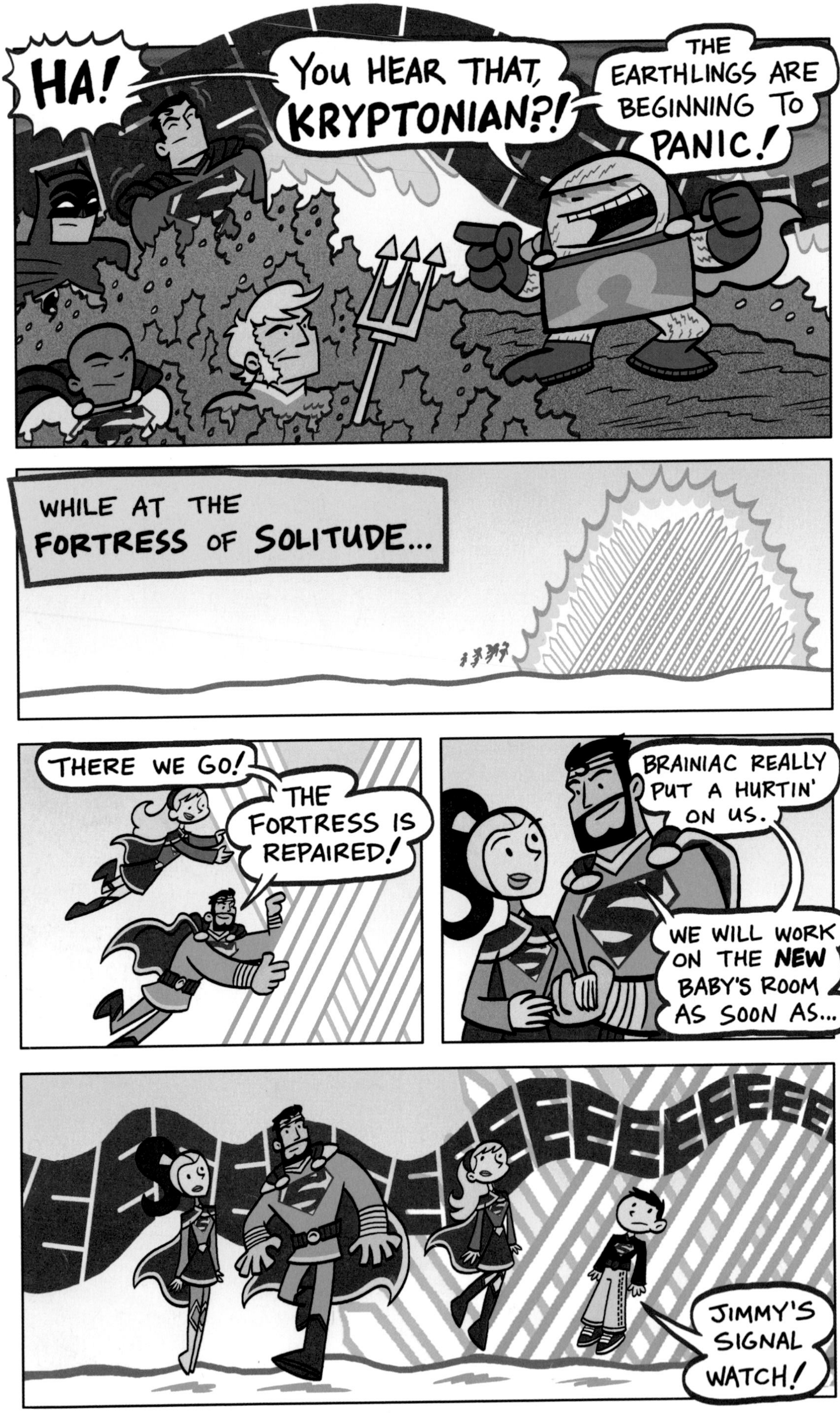
HA!
YOU HEAR THAT, KRYPTONIAN?!
THE EARTHLINGS ARE BEGINNING TO PANIC!
WHILE AT THE FORTRESS OF SOLITUDE...
THERE WE GO!
THE FORTRESS IS REPAIRED!
BRAINIAC REALLY PUT A HURTIN' ON US.
WE WILL WORK ON THE NEW BABY'S ROOM AS SOON AS...
EEEEEEEEEEEEEEEEEE
JIMMY'S SIGNAL WATCH!

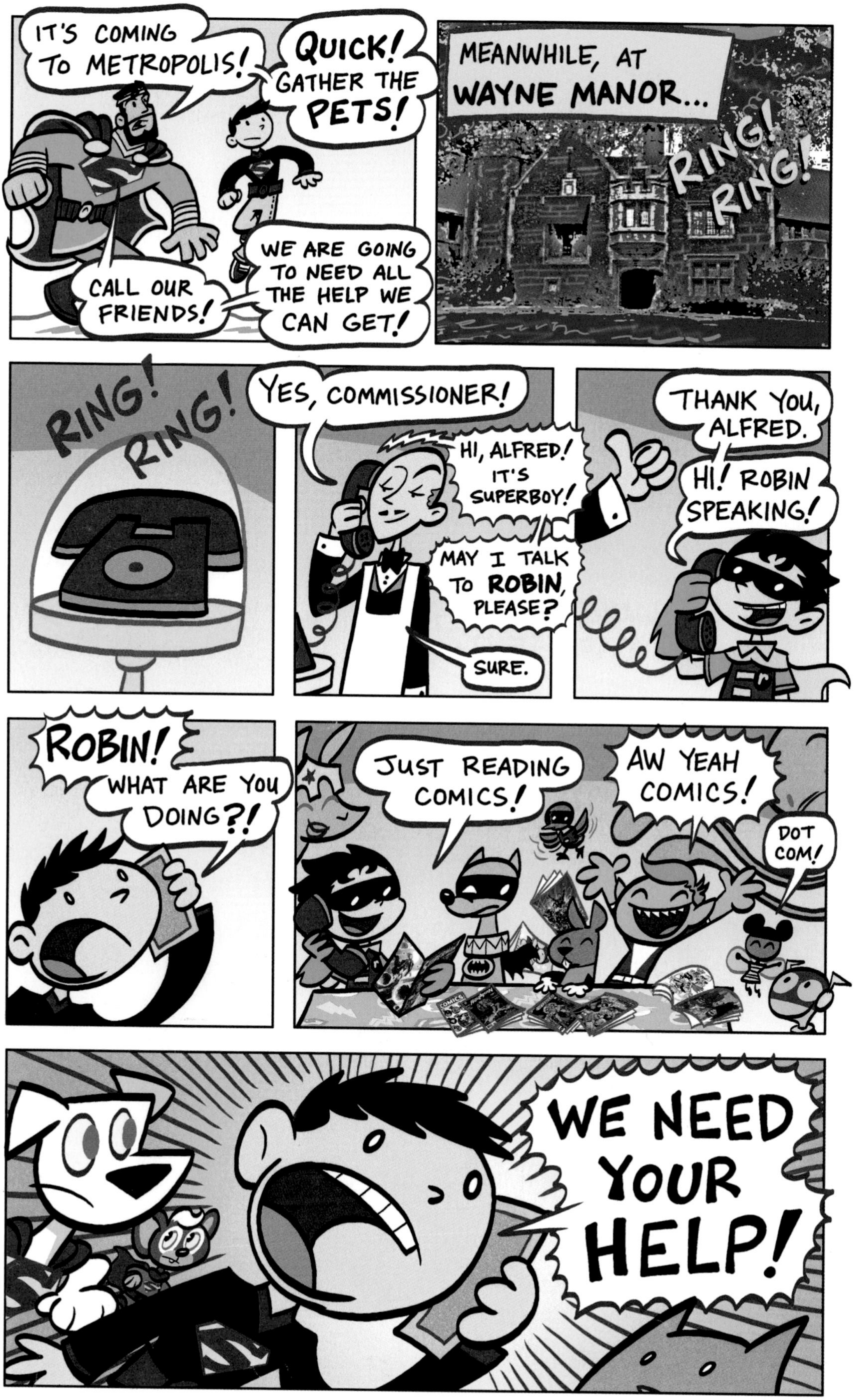
IT'S COMING TO METROPOLIS!
QUICK! GATHER THE PETS!
CALL OUR FRIENDS!
WE ARE GOING TO NEED ALL THE HELP WE CAN GET!
MEANWHILE, AT WAYNE MANOR...
RING! RING!
RING! RING!
YES, COMMISSIONER!
HI, ALFRED! IT'S SUPERBOY!
MAY I TALK TO ROBIN, PLEASE?
SURE.
THANK YOU, ALFRED.
HI! ROBIN SPEAKING!
ROBIN!
WHAT ARE YOU DOING?!
JUST READING COMICS!
AW YEAH COMICS!
DOT COM!
WE NEED YOUR HELP!

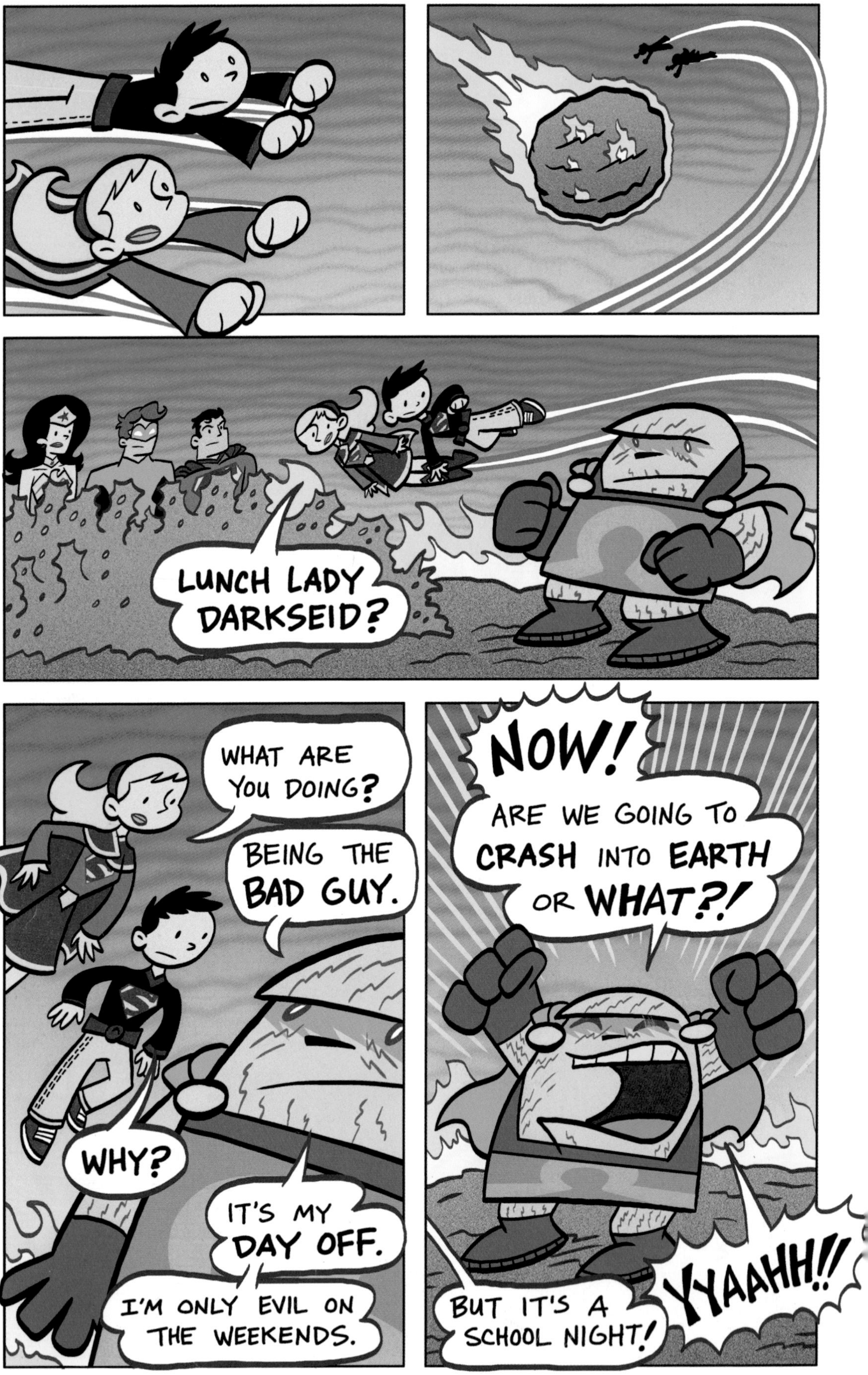
LUNCH LADY DARKSEID?
WHAT ARE YOU DOING?
BEING THE BAD GUY.
WHY?
IT'S MY DAY OFF.
I'M ONLY EVIL ON THE WEEKENDS.
NOW!
ARE WE GOING TO CRASH INTO EARTH OR WHAT?!
BUT IT'S A SCHOOL NIGHT!
YYAAHH!!

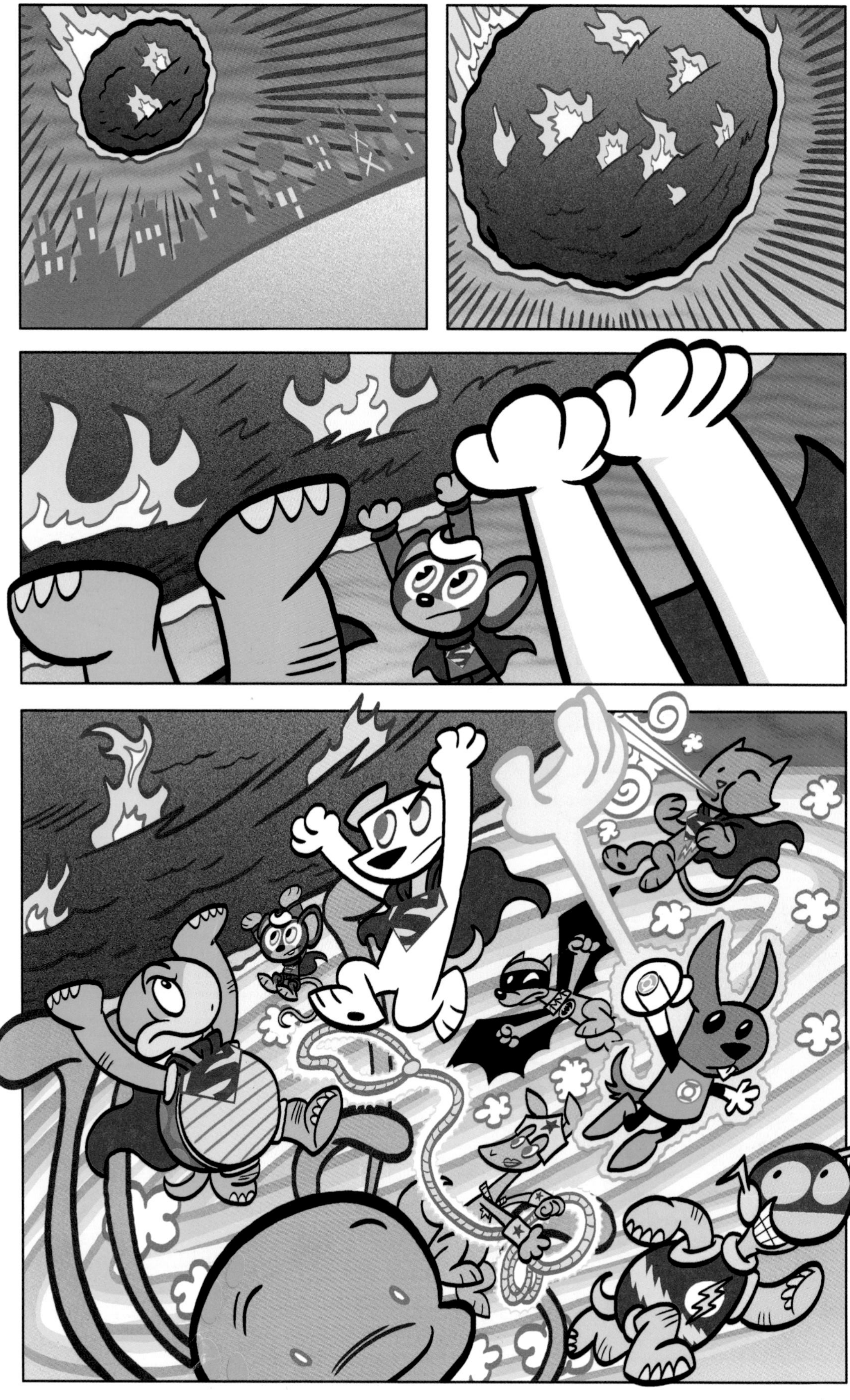

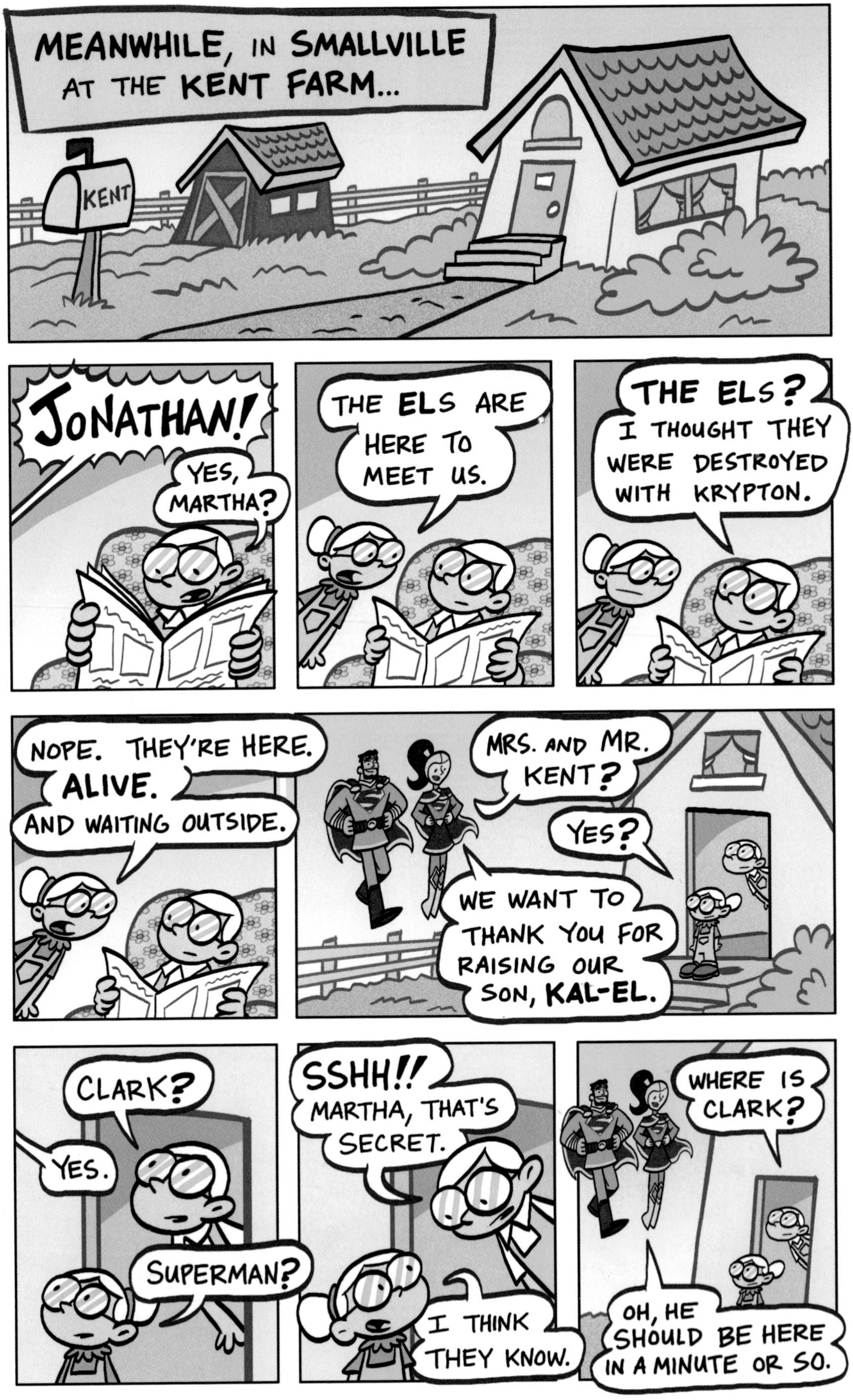
MEANWHILE, IN SMALLVILLE AT THE KENT FARM...
KENT
JONATHAN!
YES, MARTHA?
THE ELS ARE HERE TO MEET US.
THE ELS? I THOUGHT THEY WERE DESTROYED WITH KRYPTON.
NOPE. THEY'RE HERE. ALIVE. AND WAITING OUTSIDE.
MRS. AND MR. KENT?
YES?
WE WANT TO THANK YOU FOR RAISING OUR SON, KAL-EL.
CLARK?
YES.
SUPERMAN?
SSHH!! MARTHA, THAT'S SECRET.
I THINK THEY KNOW.
WHERE IS CLARK?
OH, HE SHOULD BE HERE IN A MINUTE OR SO.

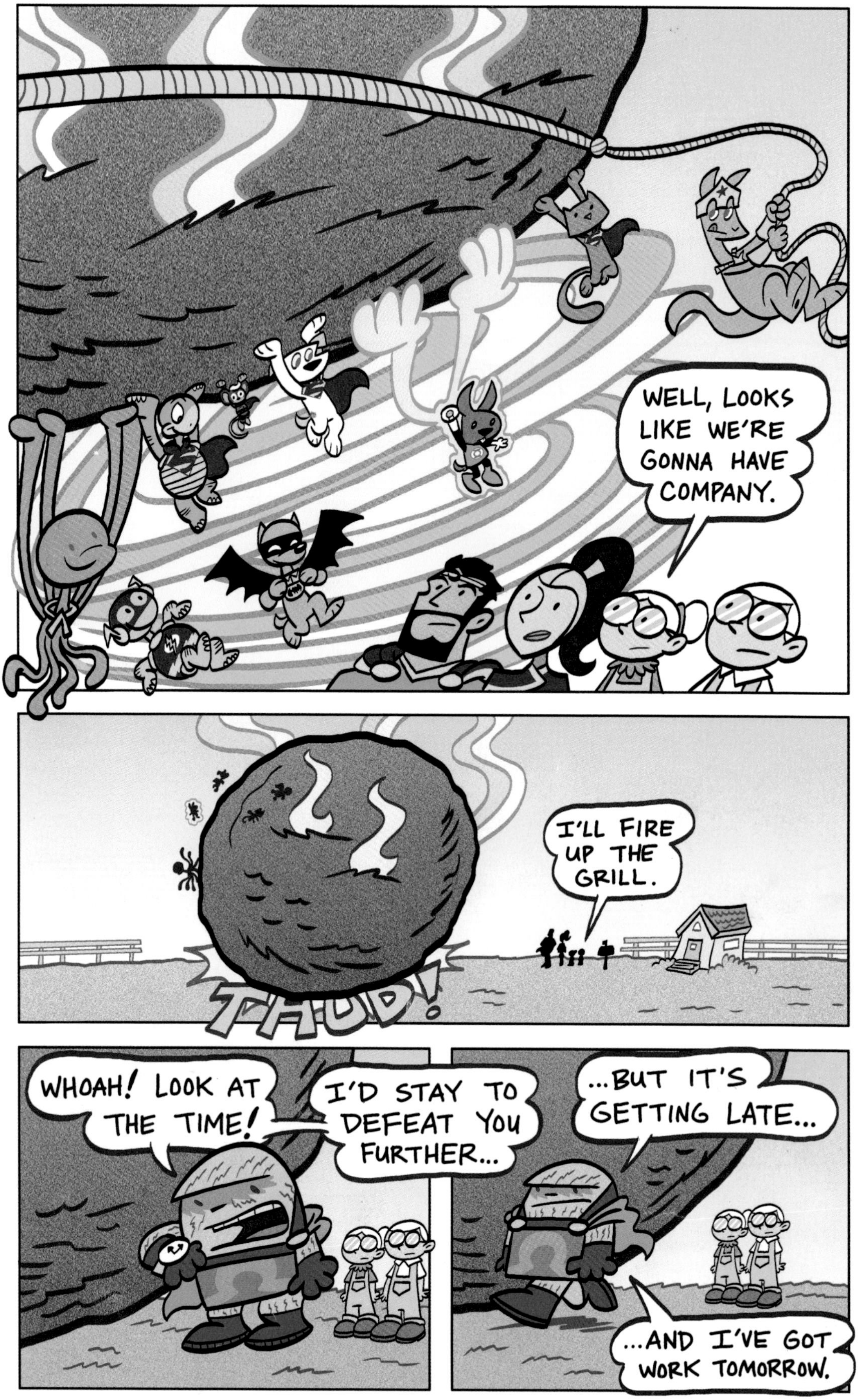
WELL, LOOKS LIKE WE'RE GONNA HAVE COMPANY.
I'LL FIRE UP THE GRILL.
THUD!
WHOAH! LOOK AT THE TIME!
I'D STAY TO DEFEAT YOU FURTHER...
...BUT IT'S GETTING LATE...
...AND I'VE GOT WORK TOMORROW.

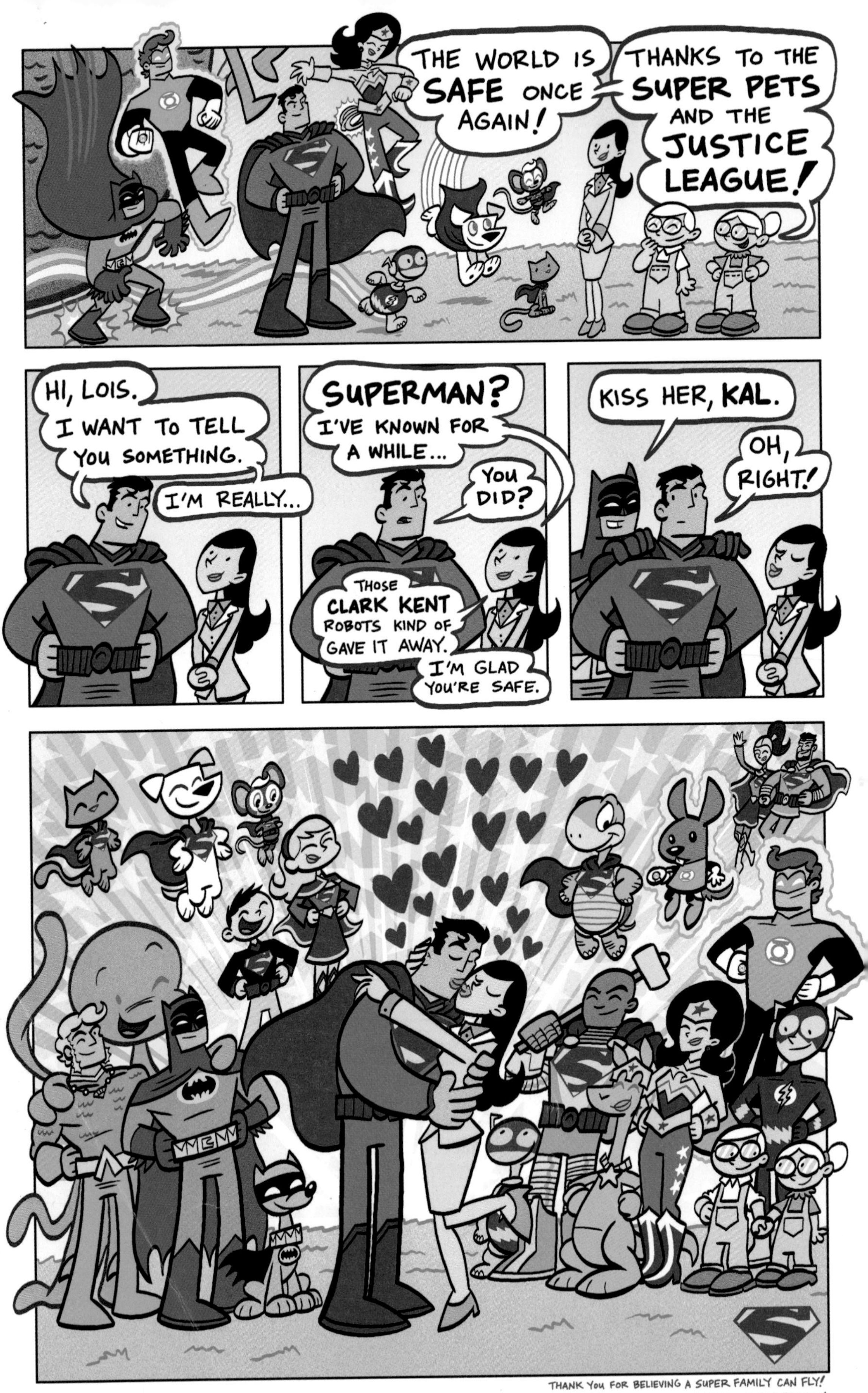
THE WORLD IS SAFE ONCE AGAIN!
THANKS TO THE SUPER PETS AND THE JUSTICE LEAGUE!
HI, LOIS. I WANT TO TELL YOU SOMETHING.
I'M REALLY...
SUPERMAN? I'VE KNOWN FOR A WHILE...
YOU DID?
THOSE CLARK KENT ROBOTS KIND OF GAVE IT AWAY.
I'M GLAD YOU'RE SAFE.
KISS HER, KAL.
OH, RIGHT!

THANK YOU FOR BELIEVING A SUPER FAMILY CAN FLY!
AW YEAH. – ART & FRANCO!

SUPERMAN®
FAMILY ADVENTURES™

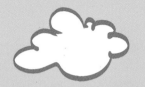

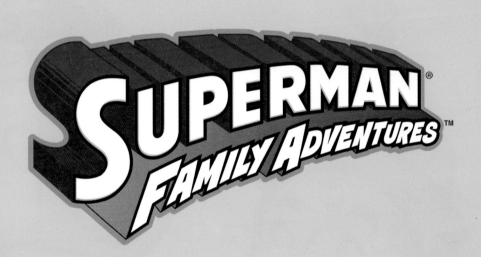

CREATORS

ART BALTAZAR IS A CARTOONIST MACHINE FROM THE HEART OF CHICAGO! HE DEFINES CARTOONS AND COMICS NOT ONLY AS AN ART STYLE, BUT AS A WAY OF LIFE. CURRENTLY, ART IS THE CREATIVE FORCE BEHIND THE NEW YORK TIMES BEST-SELLING, EISNER AWARD-WINNING, DC COMICS SERIES TINY TITANS, AND THE CO-WRITER FOR BILLY BATSON AND THE MAGIC OF SHAZAM! AND CO-CREATOR OF SUPERMAN FAMILY ADVENTURES. ART IS LIVING THE DREAM! HE DRAWS COMICS AND NEVER HAS TO LEAVE THE HOUSE. HE LIVES WITH HIS LOVELY WIFE, ROSE, BIG BOY SONNY, LITTLE BOY GORDON, AND LITTLE GIRL AUDREY. RIGHT ON!

ART BALTAZAR

FRANCO

FRANCO AURELIANI, BRONX, NEW YORK BORN WRITER AND ARTIST, HAS BEEN DRAWING COMICS SINCE HE COULD HOLD A CRAYON. CURRENTLY RESIDING IN UPSTATE NEW YORK WITH HIS WIFE, IVETTE, AND SON, NICOLAS, FRANCO SPENDS MOST OF HIS DAYS IN A BATCAVE-LIKE STUDIO WHERE HE PRODUCES DC'S TINY TITANS COMICS. IN 1995, FRANCO FOUNDED BLINDWOLF STUDIOS, AN INDEPENDENT ART STUDIO WHERE HE AND FELLOW CREATORS CAN CREATE CHILDREN'S COMICS. FRANCO IS THE CREATOR, ARTIST, AND WRITER OF WEIRDSVILLE, L'IL CREEPS, AND EAGLE ALL STAR, AS WELL AS THE CO-CREATOR AND WRITER OF PATRICK THE WOLF BOY. WHEN HE'S NOT WRITING AND DRAWING, FRANCO ALSO TEACHES HIGH SCHOOL ART.

GLOSSARY

absorption (ab-ZORP-shuhn)—the process of soaking up liquid, heat, or light

debris (duh-BREE)—the scattered pieces of something that has been broken or destroyed

disintegrate (diss-IN-tuh-grate)—to break up into small pieces

fiery (FYE-uh-ree)—hot or glowing like a fire

genius (JEEN-yuhss)—an unusually smart or talented person

intellect (IN-tuhl-ekt)—the power of the mind to think, reason, understand, and learn

lair (LAIR)—a hideaway, or a protective shelter

meteorite (MEE-tee-ur-rite)—a remaining part of a meteor that falls to Earth before it has burned up

savvy (SAV-ee)—showing quick and practical cleverness

scoop (SKOOP)—a story reported in a newspaper before other papers have a chance to report it

vast (VAST)—huge in area or extent

villain (VIL-uhn)—a wicked or evil person

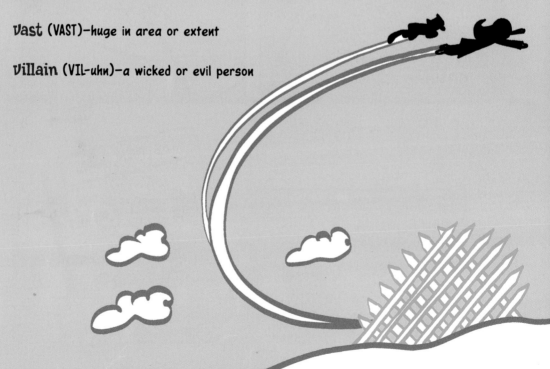

VISUAL QUESTIONS & PROMPTS

1. WHAT DO YOU THINK LEX LUTHOR'S BASE IS BUILT OUT OF? (HINT: IT WILL PROTECT HIM FROM ALL SUPER HUMANS.)

E NEED A PLACE
CAN BE SAFE
UPER BEINGS.
1

2. BASED ON WHAT YOU KNOW ABOUT THE JUSTICE LEAGUE, WHO DO YOU THINK THREW THE SEAWEED AT DARKSEID?

SPLAT
SEAWEED?
REALLY?!
2

3. BATMAN AND SUPERMAN ARE BUDDIES. IF YOU COULD HAVE A SUPER HERO FRIEND, WHICH SUPER HERO WOULD YOU CHOOSE? WHY?

KISS HER, KAL.
OH, RIGHT!
3

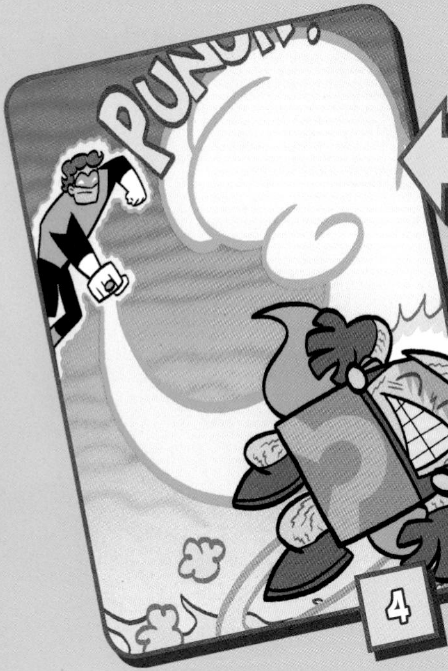
PUNCH!
4

4. GREEN LANTERN CAN USE HIS POWER RING TO CREATE CONSTRUCTS THAT DO WHATEVER HE WANTS THEM TO. WHAT ARE SOME OTHER WAYS GREEN LANTERN COULD USE HIS RING TO FIGHT DARKSEID?

5. THE JUSTICE LEAGUE ARE PROS AT WORKING TOGETHER. IDENTIFY SEVERAL PANELS IN THIS BOOK WHERE MULTIPLE SUPER HEROES HELP ACHIEVE A SHARED GOAL.

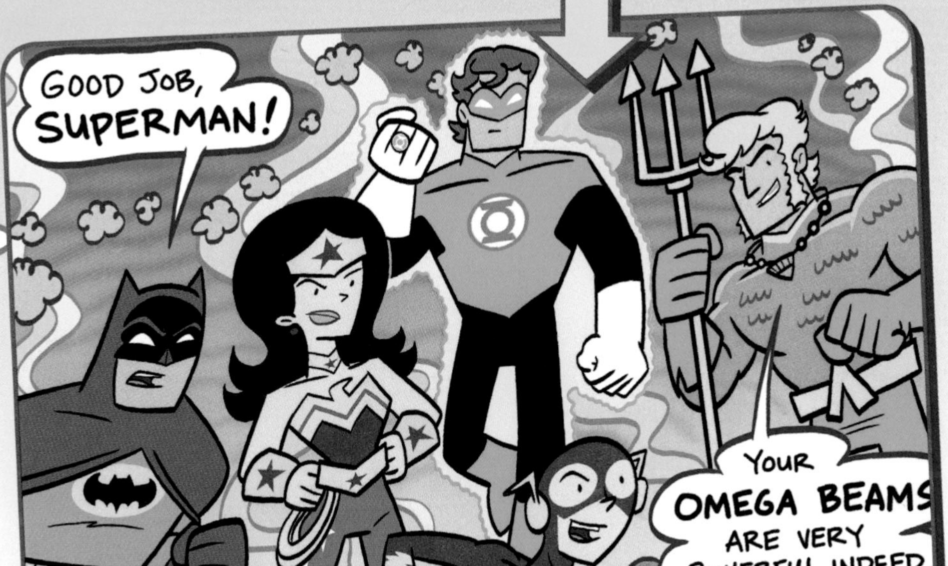
GOOD JOB, SUPERMAN!
YOUR OMEGA BEAMS ARE VERY POWERFUL INDEED, DARKSEID!
YEAH, THANKS!
5

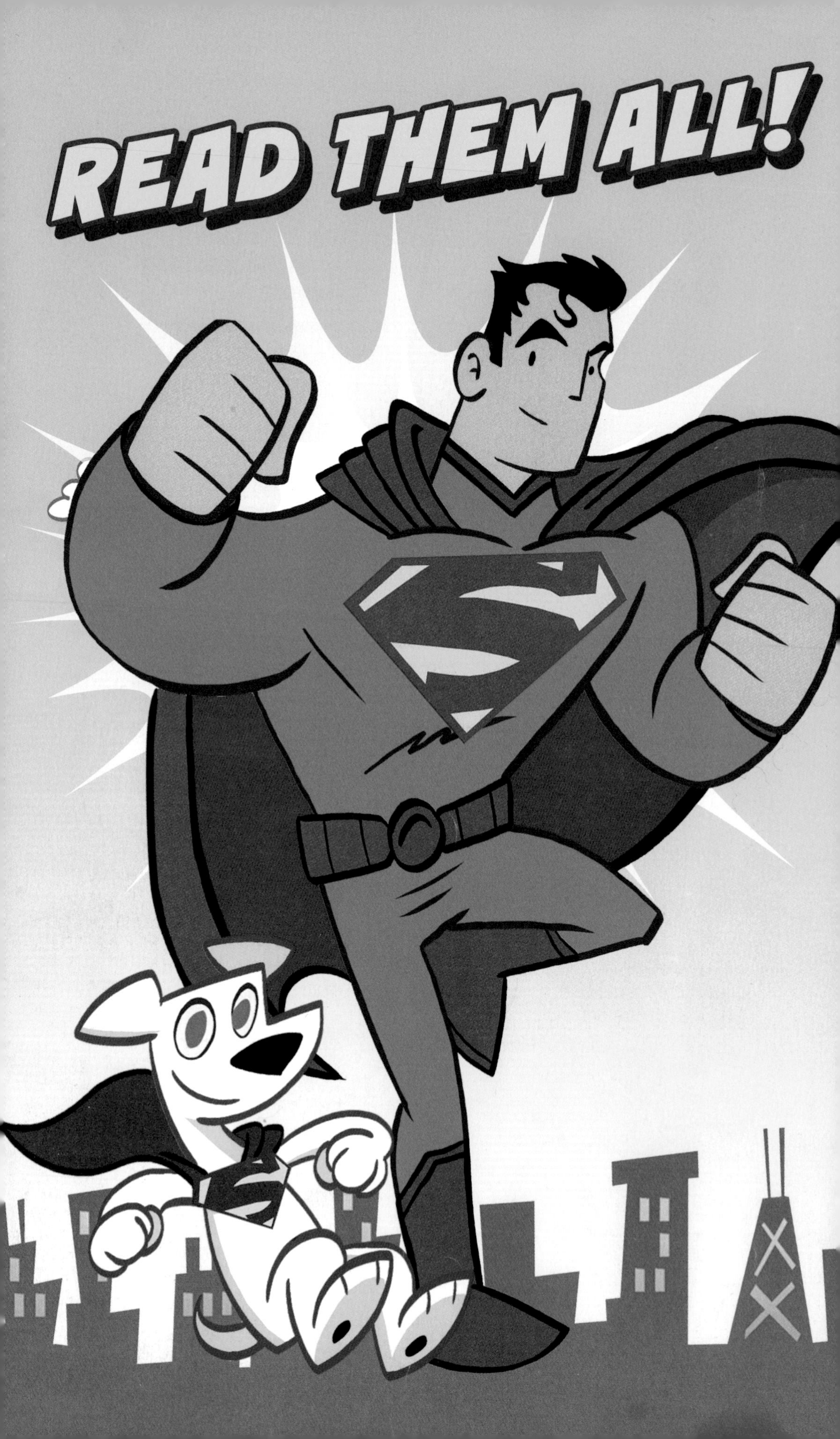
READ THEM ALL!

DAILY PLANET
SUPERMAN FAMILY ADVENTURES
ACTION FIGURES ATTACKING?!
SO MUCH FOR THAT TOOTH FAIRY PARTY!
ATTACK OF THE TOYMAN!
HA HA HA HA HA HA HA!
SUPERMAN FAMILY ADVENTURES
AND NOW... BRAINIAC!
SUPERMAN FAMILY ADVENTURES
SUPERMAN! IT'S ZOD!
GENERAL ZOD DOGS
YES. QUITE TASTY!
SUPERMAN FAMILY ADVENTURES
BECAUSE YOU DEMANDED IT
DARKSEID!
SUPERMAN FAMILY ADVENTURES
AND NOW... MA KENT!
WE'LL BE BACK FOR DINNER, MA!
OKAY. I'M MAKING SPAGHETTI!
SUPERMAN FAMILY ADVENTURES
only from...
STONE ARCH BOOKS®
a capstone imprint www.capstonepub.com

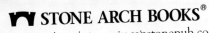

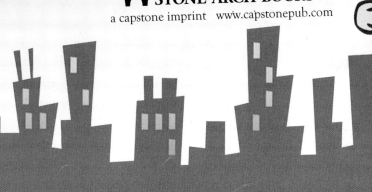

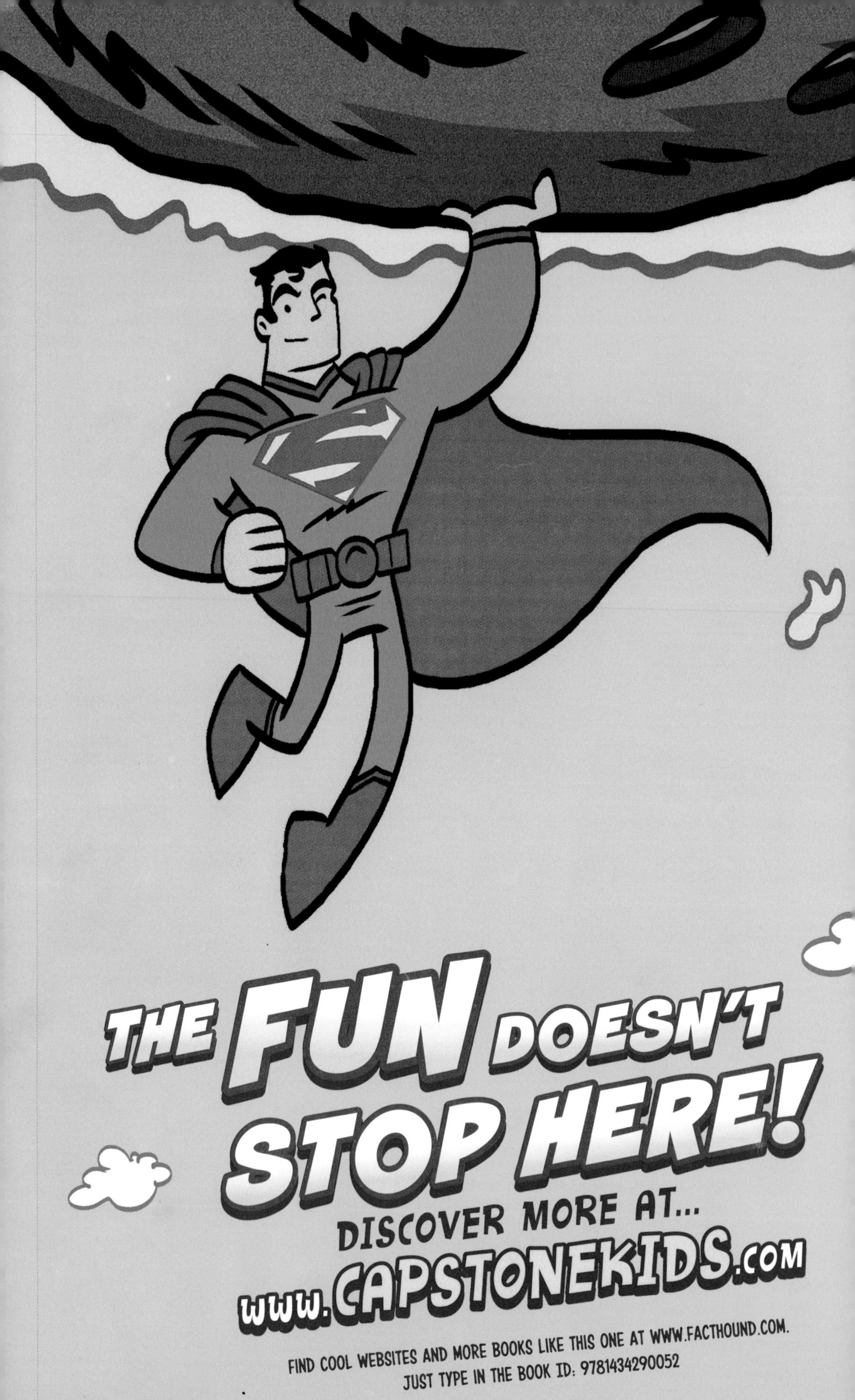

THE FUN DOESN'T STOP HERE!

DISCOVER MORE AT...

WWW.CAPSTONEKIDS.COM

FIND COOL WEBSITES AND MORE BOOKS LIKE THIS ONE AT WWW.FACTHOUND.COM.
JUST TYPE IN THE BOOK ID: 9781434290052